Bad Day for Ballet

Darcy ran out onto the stage. "Madame!" she cried. "The tape with the music for the recital is gone!"

"What?" Madame asked. "That's impossible! I put the tape into the sound system myself."

Darcy shook her head. "It's not there."

No one spoke for a moment. Then Brenda Carlton said, "I bet I know who took the tape."

Everyone turned to look at her.

"Bess Marvin!" she said loudly.

THE
NANCY DREW
NOTEBOOKS®

Bad Day for Ballet

CAROLYN KEENE
ILLUSTRATED BY ANTHONY ACCARDO

SCHOLASTIC INC.

New York Toronto London Auckland Sydney
Mexico City New Delhi Hong Kong Buenos Aires

ISBN 0-439-41982-4

12 11 10 9 8 7 6   9 10 11 12 13 14 15 16/0

Printed in the U.S.A.   40

First Scholastic printing, September 2002

Cover art by Joanie Schwarz

1

Mermaids, Pirates, and Fairies

Look at me!" said Nancy Drew. "I'm a mermaid!"

Nancy stood on tiptoe. She stretched out her arms. Then she moved them as if she were swimming.

"I'm a mermaid, too," George Fayne said.

She pretended to dive and then pop out of the water.

The two girls were standing in front of a huge mirror. The mirror covered one wall of the dance studio. They were warming up before their Friday ballet class at Madame Dugrand's Dance Academy.

George reached down and hiked up her pink tights. "Boy, I hate these things," she muttered. "They never stay up!"

Nancy grinned. She knew that George liked to wear jeans whenever she could. But Madame Dugrand had a rule. Her dance students had to wear black leotards, pink tights, and pink leather ballet slippers.

Girls with long hair had to wear it in a bun when they danced. Nancy had pinned her reddish blond hair into a bun. George had pulled her dark, curly hair into a bun, too.

Nancy pirouetted away from the mirror and glanced around the studio. More than a dozen girls were stretching and practicing dance steps. A girl with rosy cheeks and blond hair in a bun rushed in the door.

"Bess!" Nancy called to her, waving both hands. "We're over here!"

Bess Marvin waved back and hurried

across the room. Bess and George were cousins. They were also Nancy's best friends.

"Oooh," Bess moaned as soon as she reached Nancy and George. "I'm *so* nervous. I think two million butterflies are having a ballet class in my stomach."

Nancy nodded. "They're playing soccer in mine! I guess we're nervous about the dance recital on Sunday night."

"The recital." Bess gasped. "I can't even think about that. I'm nervous about tonight's dress rehearsal!"

Every year the dance academy gave a performance. This year Madame Dugrand's students were putting on "Scenes from Peter Pan." Madame had created special dances for each class. The advanced students were doing a pirates' jig. The beginners were doing Tinker Bell and the fairies. Nancy's class was dancing a mermaids' waltz.

Madame had also created solo dances. They were for the most im-

portant characters in the story—Peter Pan, Wendy, and Captain Hook.

"If you ask me, it's pretty dumb getting so nervous about a stupid recital." Someone was talking just behind Nancy's back.

Nancy whirled around. Now she was facing Brenda Carlton. Nancy knew how nasty Brenda could be.

"I don't think the recital is stupid," Nancy said. "It's fun."

Several other girls gathered around.

"Brenda's just angry," Rebecca Ramirez said.

"That's right," Jessie Shapiro added. "She's angry because she didn't get to be Wendy and dance a solo."

"That's not true!" Brenda answered. Her face turned red. "I wouldn't want that silly solo. I think it's a really stupid dance!"

"Why are you being so mean?" someone asked in a soft voice. A tall, slim girl stepped forward. She had sandy brown hair and gray eyes.

Uh-oh! Nancy thought. It's Alison Wegman.

Alison was staring at Brenda. She looked surprised and hurt.

"I thought you were my best friend," Alison went on. "But ever since Madame picked me for the Wendy solo, you won't even talk to me."

Brenda's dark brown eyes flashed. "I don't have to talk to you if I don't feel like it, Alison. And I don't feel like it!"

Brenda tossed her head. Then she marched past Alison to the far end of the studio.

Nancy glanced at Bess and George. She imagined how terrible she would feel if one of her best friends suddenly became an enemy. She tried to think of something to say to make Alison feel better.

"The Wendy solo is really beautiful," Nancy said. "Everyone thinks so. I guess Brenda's just jealous."

Alison sighed. "I wish Madame had let her dance Peter Pan or Captain Hook. But girls in the advanced classes got those solos."

"Well, I think best friends should

6

stick together no matter what," Bess said.

Just then Darcy Blair walked into the studio. She was Madame Dugrand's assistant. Darcy clapped her hands twice. Everyone stopped talking.

"To the barre!" Darcy called out.

The girls hurried to the wall opposite the big mirror. They lined up along the barre. It was a wood railing attached to the wall. The girls gripped the barre with their right hands. They stretched out their left arms, shoulder high.

Nancy stood at one end of the barre, next to the door. Bess stood just behind her, and George stood behind Bess.

Bess leaned forward and whispered to Nancy, "I really *am* scared. I missed class last week when I was sick. I don't know how to do all the steps."

"Don't worry," Nancy whispered. "We'll go over the new steps again today. You'll catch on."

Nancy felt a shiver run up her spine. She didn't know whether she was nervous or just excited. She always loved being in the dance studio. Everything about it made her feel like a real ballerina—the huge mirror, the barre, the wood floor, the piano under the tall window.

Nancy heard voices just outside the studio door. Madame Dugrand opened the door, but she didn't step inside. Nancy could see that she was talking to Jerry Cutter. Jerry was the dance academy's janitor.

"I need you Sunday night for the recital," Madame said to Jerry. "The man who was supposed to work the theater lights has the flu. You're the only other person who knows those lights."

"But it's my girlfriend's birthday." Jerry said. "I bought tickets for the Screeching Creeps concert."

"I'm sorry." Madame sighed. "I really am. I'll pay for your tickets if you can't sell them to someone else. But you *must* come on Sunday night."

"That stinks!" Jerry said. "I've already worked overtime for two weeks because of the recital." He folded his arms. After a few seconds he went on. "Okay, I'll be there on Sunday. But I just want you to know one thing. I'm really sick of this recital!"

Then Jerry Cutter stomped away.

Madame Dugrand stepped inside the studio and shut the door. She took a deep breath and walked briskly to the middle of the room.

Madame held her head high and her back straight. She wore her dark hair in a bun. She had been a ballerina onstage for many years. Then she became a ballet teacher.

Madame smiled at her students. Her blue eyes twinkled. "Remember, everyone," she said. "Dress rehearsal is here tonight at seven o'clock in the dance academy theater. We will wear costumes and makeup."

"Makeup, too," Bess whispered. "Super!"

"Super yuck!" George muttered.

Madame nodded to Darcy, who was sitting at the piano. Darcy began to play.

"Plié," Madame called out.

The girls did slow, deep knee bends. They kept their legs turned out and their backs straight. Down and up. Down and up.

Bess leaned forward again and whispered to Nancy, "I can't wait to put on our mermaid costumes. They're so beautiful!"

Madame coughed and gave Bess a stern look. Bess jumped back into position.

Madame led the class through the stretching exercises. Then the girls did low and high kicks. They held on to the barre. Their ballet slippers made swishing sounds on the wood floor.

When the music ended, Madame said, "Now we'll practice the mermaids' waltz. You must all be *perfect* mermaids by tonight's rehearsal."

The girls quickly took their places in the center of the floor. Madame put a cassette into a tape player. A friend of Madame's in Paris, France, had composed special music just for "Scenes from Peter Pan."

"Uh-oh," Bess said softly to her friends. "Just looking at that tape gives me giant goose bumps. I hope I can do all the steps."

Madame clapped her hands. The girls stood on tiptoe and lifted their arms. Nancy whispered the words "good luck" to Bess. Madame turned on the tape player. The music began.

"Very nice, girls," Madame said after a few seconds. She tapped her foot to the music. "Slide, two, three. Slide, two, three. Keep those arms curved. Remember, you are mermaids! You are swimming!"

The girls moved their arms as if they were cutting smoothly through water. They took long, even steps across the room.

"Now *glissé*—glide," Madame called out in time to the music. "Half turn and glide. Half turn and glide."

Suddenly Madame switched off the tape player. Everyone stopped dancing.

"Bess, dear," Madame said gently, "You're not keeping time. Listen to the music and move *with* it. I think you're adding an extra step."

Bess nodded. Madame rewound the tape, and the girls repeated the steps.

"Half turn and glide. Half turn and—"

Madame switched off the tape player again. She walked over to Bess and put an arm around her. "I know you can do this, Bess," she said. "Let's try it once more."

Bess's cheeks turned deep pink—pinker than her ballet tights. Her eyes met Nancy's. Nancy understood the look on her friend's face. It said, "Help!"

"Madame," Nancy said quickly, "I could do the steps in front of Bess. She could follow me."

"Good idea," Madame agreed. "Let's try it." She turned on the tape player.

Bess watched Nancy's feet. She tried to get her own feet to imitate each movement.

"Half turn and glide," Bess whispered. "Half turn and glide."

Bess did the steps correctly twice, but the third time she tripped. She stumbled backward and crashed into Brenda Carlton. Brenda crashed into Rebecca Ramirez.

"Bess!" Brenda snapped. "You are *so* clumsy!"

Bess's eyes filled with tears. "I just can't do it," she sobbed. "I hate this dance! I'd like to throw that stupid tape out the window!"

2

The Music
Is Missing

Nancy turned and put a hand on Bess's arm.

"You are *not* clumsy. I'll help you," she said.

"Me, too," George said. She glared at Brenda.

"You don't have to be so mean about everything," Rebecca told Brenda.

Madame hurried over. "Let's go on to the next part of the dance. Okay?"

"George and I can teach Bess the turns and glides," Nancy said. "We can practice with her tomorrow."

"What do you think?" Madame asked Bess.

Bess kept her eyes down, but she nodded.

Madame put the music on again. The class practiced the rest of the mermaid dance. Bess was too upset to dance her best. But she didn't make any big mistakes.

As soon as class ended, the girls raced to the dressing room to change clothes. Nancy, George, and Bess crowded into one corner.

"Do you really think you can teach me those steps?" Bess asked. She pulled on a lavender sweatshirt and matching skirt.

"I know we can," Nancy said as she finished tying her sneakers. "Even if we have to practice all day."

"All day?" Bess said. "Ick!"

"Just keep thinking about those mermaid costumes," George said. She looked down at her jeans. "Of course, *I'd* rather dance in these."

George's father drove the girls home from the dance academy. Right after dinner Bess's mother drove them back for the dress rehearsal.

They hurried through the backstage door. Voices filled the air. Nancy felt another shiver of excitement. Many of the dancers had already arrived. They were getting ready for the dress rehearsal.

Fairies lined up to have gold glitter sprinkled on their hair. Pirates tried out their cardboard swords. Darcy Blair looked over each costume. Jerry Cutter tested the stage lights.

"I love being a mermaid!" Bess said for the fourth time as Mrs. Marvin helped the girls with their makeup. "I *love* it!"

"Well, you'd better hold still, sweetie," Mrs. Marvin said. "Or you'll be the only mermaid with blue eye shadow on her nose."

Mrs. Marvin put blue eye shadow on Bess's eyelids. She brushed pink blush over her cheeks. Then she dabbed rose-colored lipstick onto Bess's lips.

"Done," she said. "Next mermaid?"

Nancy watched George duck behind

15

some scenery. "George is *not* next," Nancy said with a laugh. "So I guess I am."

Nancy managed to stand still for her makeup. But as soon as Mrs. Marvin finished, Nancy and Bess began twirling around.

Their mermaid costumes were silvery green, long-sleeved leotards and tights and silver ballet shoes. Over the leotards they wore short skirts made of soft green gauze. The fabric looked like sea water. It rippled in the air as the girls twirled.

Nancy caught sight of Alison Wegman. Alison's mother was helping Alison with her costume. Nancy stared at the shimmering, pale blue dress. It was almost ankle-length. Just above the waist it was tied with a pink satin ribbon.

"Wow!" Nancy murmured. "That's really beautiful!"

"I think it looks like a silly nightgown."

Nancy turned and saw Brenda Carlton standing next to her. Then Brenda stormed off, her gauzy mermaid costume fluttering back and forth.

"Attention, everyone!" Darcy called out. "Ten minutes to rehearsal!"

Nancy's stomach jumped the way it sometimes did in an elevator. I'll feel better if I get a drink of water, she thought.

Nancy headed toward the door that led to the main hallway. On the way she tried to find George. She peeked behind the pirate ship scenery. She looked inside the big tree that was Peter Pan's house. She didn't see George anywhere.

In the hallway Nancy got in line for the drinking fountain. Madame was standing nearby. She was talking to her six-year-old son, Paul.

"It's time to put away your toys," Madame said. "I'd like you to sit in the theater during the dress rehearsal."

Paul went on playing with his toy cars and trucks. He had spread them out all over the floor.

"I know the recital's been hard for you," Madame said. "Your baby-sitter quit. I've had to bring you here for the last few weeks. It hasn't been much fun, has it, Paul?"

Madame bent down to hug Paul. He squirmed away. She began putting his toys into the large shoe box that lay on the floor.

"Can I have money for the candy machine?" Paul asked. "I want some Hot Shots cinnamon candy."

Madame sighed. "All right. But take your toys with you. Then come right to the theater."

Paul raced down the hall, holding his toy box. Madame opened the backstage door just as Nancy finished getting her drink of water.

"Let's hurry," Madame said to Nancy.

Backstage, Darcy Blair stood on a tall stool. She clapped her hands. The noise died down.

"The dress rehearsal is about to begin!" Darcy announced. "We'd like everyone except dancers to leave the theater. Madame Dugrand wants the recital to be a surprise. She thanks all of you for your help with the costumes and makeup.''

Two minutes later only the dancers, Madame, and Darcy remained backstage.

"We're ready for the opening dance,'' Madame called. "Everyone onstage. Pirates first. Then fairies and mermaids.''

The girls filed onstage between panels of the heavy curtains. Nancy, Bess, and George waited with the other mermaids.

"Where did you hide?'' Nancy asked George.

George smiled. "Top secret!''

"Mermaids, onstage!'' Darcy called out.

As the mermaids began moving toward the stage, Bess glanced down at her tights. She saw a pale line running down one leg.

"What's that?'' she said. She bent over to examine it. "Oh, no! My tights are ripped.'' She slipped off her ballet shoe. She found a hole in the toe of her tights.

"Bess! Brenda! What's taking so long?''

Bess looked up. The other mermaids had gone. Darcy was waiting by the curtain. Brenda was standing near her dance bag. She was putting a barrette in her hair.

"I'm trying to hurry," Brenda said. "My barrette fell out." She fastened the clip and dashed past Darcy.

"Come on, Bess," said Darcy. Then she walked onto the stage.

Bess pulled on her ballet shoe and followed Darcy.

All the dancers were in position. Bess slipped into her place behind Nancy.

Nancy turned and smiled at her friend. Then she looked toward the front of the stage. She saw rows and rows of seats. Her stomach jumped again. The theater looked so big! The stage felt so high! Nancy took a deep breath.

Madame studied the large group of dancers. She shook her head. "Pirates move two steps to the left." She showed them where to stand.

"Okay, everybody. Arms straight," Madame called out. "Fairies, keep your toes pointed. Good, I think we're ready for the music."

A door slammed. Nancy glanced around the theater. Paul was walking down the center aisle. He had a small box of candy in one hand. Under his other arm he carried the toy box and a comic book. He sat down in the second row. He opened the candy and began reading the comic book.

Madame nodded to Darcy. "The tape is in the sound system backstage," she said. "On the count of three, begin the music."

Darcy went backstage. Madame took one last look at the dancers. Then she tapped her foot and counted. "One. Two. Three!"

There was complete silence. Seconds passed. No one moved.

Madame frowned and tapped her foot again. "One. Two. *Three!*"

Suddenly Darcy ran out onto the stage. She looked pale.

"Madame!" she cried. "The tape is gone!"

3

Friends Stick Together

What?" Madame asked. "That's impossible! I put the tape into the sound system myself just a half hour ago!"

Darcy shook her head. "It's not there. I looked all around the sound system. The tape is gone."

No one spoke for a moment. Then Brenda Carlton said, "I bet I know who took the tape." Everyone turned to look at her. "Bess Marvin!" she said loudly.

Bess gasped.

Madame turned to Brenda. "How can you say such a thing?"

Brenda put her hands on her hips. "Bess was the last one backstage," she said. "I saw her there. Darcy did, too. And everyone heard what Bess said this afternoon. She said she hated the dance. She said she wanted to throw the tape out the window."

Bess's eyes and mouth opened wide. But she didn't say a word. She kept staring at Brenda.

"Bess didn't take the tape," Nancy said. "I *know* she didn't."

"Bess would never do something like that!" George exclaimed.

"I *was* the last one backstage," Bess said. "But I didn't touch the tape." Her eyes filled with tears. She blinked hard to keep from crying.

Madame looked at Brenda. "The tape has probably just been put in the wrong place. I don't think anybody took it. I'll look for it myself."

Madame hurried backstage. Nancy and George stood close to Bess.

Darcy came over and handed Bess a

tissue. "The tape's bound to turn up," she said gently.

"I'll find it," Nancy whispered to Bess. "I promise! I've solved other mysteries."

Bess looked at Nancy and George and tried to smile. "Friends stick together, right?"

"Right," said George.

Madame returned, looking very worried. "I can't find the tape anywhere," she said. She walked to the front of the stage to face the students. "I put the tape into the sound system myself. So someone *must* have taken it out. I don't know who did this. I won't accuse anyone."

Nancy glanced around. She saw Alison, Rebecca, and Jessie watching Bess.

Madame went on. "The tape can't be replaced. So there's only one thing I can do. I will be in my office tomorrow and Sunday. I would like whoever took the tape to return it to me. No questions will be asked."

"What about the dress rehearsal?" one of the older dancers asked.

Madame shook her head. "We can't dance without the music. But I want all of you to be here at three o'clock on Sunday. If the tape has been returned, we'll rehearse at three. If there's no tape—" Madame paused and looked at the girls. "Then at three o'clock I will cancel Sunday night's recital."

Alison looked as though she was about to cry. "What about my solo?" she blurted out. "It's not fair!"

"It's not fair for any of us," said Madame. Then she left the stage to get Paul. Darcy led the girls backstage to the dressing room. Nancy, George, and Bess walked at the end of the line. Nancy noticed other girls whispering and looking at Bess.

"Go ahead without me," Nancy told her friends. "I want to look around here."

"I'm sticking with you," George said.

"Me, too," Bess said.

The three girls hid behind the big tree that was Peter Pan's house. They waited until everyone else was gone.

Stepping out from behind the tree,

Nancy said, "Look for the tape and anything else that might be a clue. We've got to hurry!"

George searched near the curtain and the lights. Bess checked the scenery and props.

Nancy looked at the sound system. "No clues," she muttered. "Not even half a clue!"

Then she checked around the sound system. There was something lying on the floor. She reached for it.

Nancy felt someone grab her shoulder. She whirled around. It was George.

"We'd better get out of here," George said.

Nancy nodded and waved for Bess to come over. Then she held out her hand. On her palm lay a small silver object about two and a half inches long. It came to a point at one end.

"An Eiffel Tower charm," Bess said.

"Madame got a bunch of them in France," George said. "She told us that they're just like the real Eiffel Tower in Paris."

"And she gives them out as prizes for really good work," Bess added.

"Right," Nancy said. "And so far she's given one to Alison and one to Brenda."

Just then they heard rapid footsteps crossing the backstage. Jerry Cutter came toward them, frowning.

"What are you kids doing near the sound system? I nearly turned off the lights and locked you in."

"We were looking for the tape," Nancy said. "We're going now."

Nancy, Bess, and George ran back to the dressing room. They went to their corner to change out of their costumes.

"Do you want to practice the mermaid dance tomorrow afternoon?" George asked. She pulled off her ballet shoes. "We could do it at Bess's house."

"Sure," Nancy said. "What do you think, Bess?"

Bess nodded. She was carefully folding her silvery green tights and leotard into her dance bag.

"If we can't find the tape, no one will get to be a mermaid," she whispered sadly. "And everyone will think it's my fault."

"We *will* find the tape," Nancy said.

"But how?" Bess asked. "There are no clues."

"We *do* have a clue," Nancy said. She glanced around the dressing room. The other girls had already left. Nancy showed Bess and George the Eiffel Tower charm again.

"That's a clue?" George asked. "What does it have to do with the missing tape?"

"This might be a really big clue," Nancy said in a low voice. "It's given me an idea. An idea about who could have taken the tape."

"Who?" Bess asked.

Nancy's fingers closed tightly around the little Eiffel Tower. She looked at her friends and said, "Brenda Carlton!"

4

Pancakes
and Ice Cream

Brenda!" Bess gasped. "Why would *she* take the tape?"

"Here's what I think," Nancy said. "Brenda was super angry that Madame gave the Wendy solo to Alison. Brenda wanted to get back at Madame. She wanted to keep Alison from being the star, too. So she took the tape. Then she tried to blame Bess."

"When did she do it?" George asked.

"She was the last one backstage tonight except for Bess and Darcy,"

Nancy explained. "Maybe she took the tape and put it in her dance bag when Darcy wasn't looking."

"That's right!" Bess said. "I saw her standing next to her dance bag."

"If this Eiffel Tower charm is Brenda's," Nancy went on, "maybe she lost it when she took the tape."

George nodded. "Brenda's such a show-off. She *always* wears her charm."

"On a silver chain around her neck," Bess added.

"Now I need more clues to prove it," said Nancy. She glanced at the clock on the wall. "Oops. We'd better get going. My dad will be here any minute to drive us home."

Nancy put the charm in her jacket pocket. Then the girls picked up their dance bags and hurried out of the dressing room.

That night, after she was tucked in bed, Nancy thought about the missing tape. Words kept running through her mind. Recital. Music. Mermaid dance. Wendy's solo.

Nancy leaned over and switched on the lamp. She opened the drawer in her bedside table and took out a red pen and a small notebook with a shiny blue cover. It was her detective's notebook. In it she wrote about each of her cases.

Nancy turned to a clean page. On the top line she wrote: "The Ballet Mystery." On the next two lines, she wrote two questions:

Who wants to stop the recital?
Who was backstage and had a chance to take the tape?

Below the questions, Nancy wrote two words: "Brenda Carlton."

Nancy flipped to the next page. On the top line she wrote: "Clues." Just below that she drew a picture of the Eiffel Tower. Then she put the notebook and pen on the table. She switched off the light. A minute later she was fast asleep.

The next morning Nancy washed up and put on jeans and a yellow sweater.

She grabbed her notebook and pen and ran downstairs to the kitchen.

The sun was shining through the big window over the sink. Her father, Carson Drew, was beating eggs in a bowl.

"It's Signorina Ballerina!" he said when he saw Nancy. "How many banana pancakes can she eat today? Twenty-two? Thirty-five?"

Nancy laughed. Saturday mornings were special. Hannah Gruen, the family housekeeper, usually went out. She had been living with the Drews since Nancy was three years old. That was when Nancy's mother had died.

Nancy loved Hannah very much. But she also loved Saturday breakfast with just her father. He made great pancakes. And they had lots of time to talk.

"How about three pancakes?" Nancy asked.

Mr. Drew sighed. He pretended to be disappointed. "If you insist. But three doesn't seem like much for a ballerina. Especially one who has a mystery to solve."

Nancy had told her father all about the missing tape the night before.

While Mr. Drew sliced bananas, Nancy finished mixing the batter. Then she set the table while he flipped pancakes in the big frying pan. After they sat down to eat, Nancy showed her father her notebook.

"You're asking the right questions," he said. "But let's go over them again." Carson Drew was a lawyer. He knew all about mysteries and crimes. "Did anyone *besides* Brenda want to stop the recital?" he asked. "Did anyone else have a chance to take the tape?"

Nancy put a bite of banana pancake in her mouth. She chewed slowly and thought. She started to take another bite. Her fork stopped in midair.

"Yes!" she said. "There *is* someone else! Jerry Cutter, the janitor. He wanted to take his girlfriend to a concert on Sunday. He was really angry about having to be at the recital. And he was working backstage last night!"

"Good thinking, Signorina Ballerina!" Carson Drew grinned with pride.

Nancy wiped her fingers on her napkin and picked up the notebook. On the line below Brenda's name, she wrote: Jerry Cutter.

Nancy and her father washed the breakfast dishes. Then they put a new bell on Nancy's blue bike. Nancy spent the rest of the morning reading a library book. But she found it hard to pay attention. She kept thinking, I have to find the tape by three o'clock tomorrow!

When Hannah got back, she made Nancy tuna salad for lunch. After lunch Nancy biked over to Bess's house. She carried her ballet slippers and notebook in her backpack. When she got to Bess's house, George's red bike was already leaning against the front steps.

"You're finally here," Bess said as she opened the door. "Wait till you see what I've got." Bess led the way to the living room.

"Look!" she said, pointing to the coffee table.

Nancy saw tubes of lipstick, a blush compact, and some green eye shadow. Bess was holding a large hand mirror.

"My mom gave me the makeup," Bess explained. "She said we could practice with it. I think good makeup is just as important as good dancing."

"Give me a break!" someone muttered.

Nancy glanced around the room. She saw George's dark curls poking over the top of an armchair. The chair had been turned to the wall.

George leaned around the side of the chair. She was holding a comic book. "Watch out," she said to Nancy. "Or Bess will rub that goop all over your face."

Nancy laughed. She picked up one of the lipsticks. It would be fun to play with the makeup. But they had to practice the dance.

"I've got an idea," Nancy said to Bess. "Let's spend ten minutes doing makeup. Then we'll dance until you learn the steps."

"Ten minutes!" George groaned. "The longest ten minutes of my life!"

Nancy tried two of the lipsticks. Bess made her cheeks bright red with blush. George kept as far away from the makeup as possible. She moved chairs and small tables to the side of the room. She kept checking her watch.

"Bong!" George yelled. "Time's up!"

The three girls began practicing the mermaids' waltz. Nancy did the steps in front of Bess. Bess tried to follow her. George watched Bess and tried to catch mistakes. She also tried to hum the mermaid music.

Bess wrinkled her nose and put her hands over her ears. "That music sounds pretty weird," she said.

George shrugged. "I guess I'm not a very good singer."

Nancy giggled. "Maybe you could just clap the time the way Madame does."

The girls went over the steps again and again. At the end of an hour Bess could do the dance with very few mistakes.

"Time for a break," Bess said. She flopped onto the sofa.

"Hey," George protested, "I was just getting warmed up."

Bess moaned. "How about cooling off? With a chocolate ripple ice cream cone. We could bike down to Sugar 'n' Spice."

Mrs. Marvin gave them permission—after the lipstick and blush were washed off. The girls jumped on their bikes and headed toward Sugar 'n' Spice, four blocks away. It was their favorite ice cream shop.

As they pedaled, Nancy told Bess and George about Jerry Cutter. "He might have taken the tape," Nancy explained. "But I think Brenda is a better suspect."

George agreed. "We have a clue for Brenda—the Eiffel Tower charm."

The girls turned a corner.

"This is Brenda's street," Bess said.

Just then the door to Brenda's house opened. Brenda and her mother walked out. Mrs. Carlton smiled and waved to Nancy, Bess, and George. She began loading some packages into the trunk of her car.

Nancy braked her bike near Brenda. Bess and George did the same.

"Are you going shopping?" Nancy asked. She tried to sound friendly.

Brenda shrugged. "My mom has errands to do. I'm supposed to get my hair trimmed for the recital." Then she stared at Bess. *"If* there's a recital."

Bess's cheeks turned deep pink.

Brenda kicked a pebble with the toe of her loafer. "Whoever took that tape should just return it," she said.

"We think so, too," Nancy answered quickly.

Nancy and Brenda glared at each other.

"Brenda, time to go!" Mrs. Carlton called.

Brenda turned and ran to the car. Nancy, Bess, and George got back on their bikes and rode down the street.

As soon as they turned the next corner, Nancy asked, "Did you two notice something?" She sounded excited.

"Notice what?" George asked.

"A clue?" Bess said.

The girls braked their bikes.

"What are you talking about, Nancy?" George asked.

Nancy's eyes gleamed. "I'm talking about Brenda," she said. "Brenda was missing something. Something important. Her Eiffel Tower charm!"

5

The Silver Clue

George gave a low whistle. "Wow! You mean Brenda wasn't wearing it."

Nancy shook her head. "I've never, ever seen Brenda without her charm. But she didn't have it today." Nancy tapped her fingers on the handlebars of her bike. "We still need real proof that Brenda took the tape."

George nodded and looked at her watch. "Guess what? We have exactly twenty-four hours. It's three o'clock."

"Ooooh," Bess moaned, putting her hands over her stomach. "I'm so worried I think I've lost my appetite—almost."

"Almost!" Nancy and George repeated, laughing.

The girls rode on to Sugar 'n' Spice. They each bought a chocolate ripple cone dipped in candy sprinkles. Then they stood outside the shop. They leaned against their bikes and ate.

"Can you hold my cone for a second?" Nancy asked. George took the cone. Nancy got her notebook and pen out of her backpack. She flipped to the page labeled Clues.

Bess looked over Nancy's shoulder. She pointed to the drawing of the Eiffel Tower. "Goo pictha uh da Eiffo Towa," she said. Her mouth was full of ice cream.

Nancy laughed and imitated Bess. "Tha koo for saying my picture is good!"

Under the picture Nancy wrote: "Saturday afternoon. Brenda doesn't have her charm."

The girls finished their ice cream and biked back to Bess's house. They practiced the dance once more. Then George and Nancy biked home.

After dinner that evening Carson Drew said to Nancy, "I have a little work to do. Can you stay out of trouble for an hour or so?"

"I can for an hour," Nancy said. "But after that you have to read to me. You promised."

"And I always keep my promises," Mr. Drew said in his deepest voice.

Nancy gave her father a big hug and went upstairs to her bedroom. She got out her crayons and a new, very special coloring book from France. Madame Dugrand had given one to each girl in Nancy's class.

Nancy sat on the floor and looked at the pictures. The book was about a French girl named Marie. She was just Nancy's age and took ballet lessons in Paris.

Nancy picked a picture of Paris to color. It went across two pages. In it Marie stood looking at the Eiffel Tower. The tower looked just like the charms Madame had brought back from Paris.

Nancy picked out a yellow crayon

and a red one. She wanted to make Marie's hair the same color as her own. She made Marie's dress light blue. That was Nancy's favorite color. She made the buildings of Paris gray and tan, just as in the photographs Madame had showed them. Next she did the sky. She pressed hard with a bright blue crayon. The crayon snapped in two.

"Phooey!" Nancy muttered. She heard footsteps in the hallway.

"Anything wrong, Pumpkin?" asked Carson Drew. He stepped into the room and saw her picture. "Nice work!" he said.

"But my sky blue crayon just broke." Nancy sighed. "And I'm running out of red."

"How about some new crayons?" Mr. Drew asked. "We'll go to the mall tomorrow morning. Toy store for you and bookstore for me."

Nancy grinned. "Is that a promise?"

Nancy woke up early the next morning and stared at her clock. Eight A.M., she thought. Just seven hours left!

Nancy jumped out of bed and washed up. She was finishing breakfast an hour later when the phone rang. It was Bess. The girls made plans to meet at the mall. Bess's mother had some shopping to do, and Bess needed a new pair of tights for her mermaid costume.

At ten o'clock Nancy and her father walked into the toy store. Mr. Drew stopped to look at some model ships. Nancy went looking for crayons.

As she turned down a long aisle, she saw Alison Wegman. Alison was with her older sister. Nancy noticed Alison's Eiffel Tower charm right away. It was hanging from her belt.

"Hi, Alison," Nancy said.

Alison smiled. "Hi, Nancy." Then her smile faded. "Did you hear? The tape hasn't been returned. Brenda's mother called Madame Dugrand this morning. Then Brenda called me."

Nancy was surprised. "I thought you and Brenda were enemies."

Alison shook her head. "Not any-more. Brenda asked to make up and be best friends again. I said okay. I wasn't

46

the one who wanted to fight." Alison's face brightened. "We're going to shop for clothes for our ballerina dolls. There's Brenda now!"

Nancy turned around. Brenda was walking toward them.

"Hi, Brenda," Nancy said.

"Oh, hi," said Brenda. She didn't smile.

No one spoke for a moment.

Finally Nancy said, "Well, have a good time shopping for doll clothes."

Something shiny caught Nancy's eye. She looked down at Brenda's open jacket. Just inside the jacket was a silver chain.

Oh, no! Nancy thought.

Dangling from the chain was an Eiffel Tower charm!

6

Who Did It?

Nancy froze for a second. Then she managed to choke out the words, "See you later." She turned and ran up the aisle to the crayon display.

As soon as Mr. Drew had paid for Nancy's new crayons, they walked to the dance shop.

"Have fun," Mr. Drew said. "When you're done, Mrs. Marvin can bring you to the bookstore. Look for me under Mysteries."

Carson Drew winked at his daughter. Nancy tried to smile, but she felt too upset. She knew now that Brenda had not taken the tape. At three o'clock Madame would cancel the recital. How could she solve the mystery by then?

Nancy opened the door to the shop. Mrs. Marvin was just stepping into a dressing room. Bess was at a counter, looking at tights.

"Nancy, don't you love this color?" Bess held up a pair of turquoise tights. "They'd be so cute with my turquoise jumper."

Then Bess sighed. "But I can't get them. My mom says new mermaid tights are enough for one day. But aren't these cool?"

Nancy barely looked at the tights. She took a deep breath and said, "Bess, I have something *really* important to tell you."

Bess stared at Nancy. "What?"

"Bad news," Nancy said. "I just saw Brenda and Alison in the toy shop. They're best friends again. And they were both wearing their Eiffel Tower charms."

Bess dropped the turquoise tights

back on the counter. She stood very still.

Nancy continued. "That means Brenda isn't a good suspect. Maybe she wasn't all that mad at Alison. At least not mad enough to steal the tape and ruin the recital. And she didn't drop her charm near the sound system. I don't know whose charm I found. I guess it's just one of Madame's."

Bess turned away. She looked down at the turquoise tights.

"I should just buy these," she said. Her voice shook. "We're not going to find the tape. The recital's going to be canceled. And everyone's going to think I'm a thief." Her eyes filled with tears.

Nancy put her arm around Bess. "Remember—friends stick together. I'm going to solve this mystery. There's still another suspect—Jerry Cutter. Hannah can take me to the academy early to look for more clues. I'll find something."

Nancy tried to comfort Bess. But she was worried. She worried the rest of the time at the mall. She worried on the drive home.

As soon as she walked into the house, Nancy got out her blue notebook. She drew a red line through Brenda's name. She drew a red circle around Jerry Cutter's name. Then she went into the kitchen.

Hannah was at the sink, washing tomatoes. Nancy began handing her the unwashed ones.

"Hannah," Nancy asked, "could you take me to the dance academy early this afternoon? I want to look for something. And talk to Madame Dugrand."

Hannah raised her eyebrows. Her eyes twinkled. "This sounds very mysterious. I think I can get you there by two-fifteen."

Nancy put her arm around Hannah's waist. "Thanks," she said.

At exactly two-fifteen Nancy walked into the academy. Just forty-five minutes to go, she thought. The straps of her dance bag were slung over her shoulder. Inside the bag were her costume, hairbrush, notebook, pen, and the Eiffel Tower charm.

The door to Madame Dugrand's office was half open. "Madame," Nancy said. She pushed the door a little. "Can I talk to you?"

Madame looked up from her desk. "Are you here about the tape?" she asked.

"Yes," Nancy said.

Madame suddenly looked sad. "I promised I wouldn't ask any questions, but I just can't understand why you took that tape."

Nancy gasped. Madame thought she had come to return the stolen tape! How awful it felt to have someone think she was a thief. How awful Bess must feel!

"I didn't take the tape!" Nancy cried. "I'm just looking for it!"

Madame folded her hands on her desk. "Well," she said, "I couldn't believe you'd ever take anything."

Nancy shook her head. "I just want to prove that Bess Marvin is innocent. And I want to save the recital."

Madame sighed deeply. "I'm afraid the recital is lost, dear. Whoever took the tape would have returned it by now."

"Is anyone else in the building?" Nancy asked.

"Just Paul and Jerry Cutter," Madame said. "Paul is right down the hall with his toys."

"May I look around?" Nancy asked.

Madame nodded and went back to her work.

Nancy checked the big clock at the end of the hallway. Twenty-five minutes past two! She headed quickly for the supply room. Jerry Cutter used the room as his office.

The door was open. "Jerry?" Nancy called. She stepped inside to talk to the janitor.

He wasn't there. Nancy looked around the room. Shelves were piled high with cleaning supplies. A ladder leaned against the wall. There were buckets, brooms, and stacks of lumber.

Something on one of the shelves caught Nancy's eye. She stepped closer

to look. It was a tape cassette! It was leaning against a box.

Nancy reached for the tape. Just then she heard footsteps coming down the hall. It must be Jerry, she thought. She crouched behind a big carton and held her breath.

The footsteps entered the room. Nancy heard papers rustling. Then she heard footsteps near the door.

Suddenly the lights went out. The door slammed shut!

7

A New Clue

Nancy's heart pounded. The room was pitch-black. Find the light switch, she told herself.

Nancy stood up and stepped carefully in the direction of the wall. She held out her hands until she touched some shelves. Then she felt her way along the shelves to the light switch near the door.

Nancy flipped the switch. Light flooded the room. She ran back to the low shelf and grabbed the tape. The picture on the label showed four rock singers with green hair. The tape was

"The Screeching Creeps Greatest Hits."

"Creeps is right," Nancy muttered. She put the tape back on the shelf. Then she switched off the light and left the office.

Holding her dance bag on her shoulder, Nancy ran up the hallway. She looked at the clock. Two thirty-five. Just twenty-five more minutes! Time seemed to be passing faster and faster.

Nancy jogged around the corner. She nearly tripped over one of Paul Dugrand's toy cars.

"Sorry!" Nancy panted.

"Want to see how fast this car goes?" Paul asked. He sent a tiny car racing between two toy buildings. "Zoom!" he shouted.

Nancy stared at Paul's toys. He had set up a little city. He had toy buildings, street signs, traffic lights, and lots of tiny cars.

"It looks so familiar," Nancy said. She couldn't take her eyes off the scene. Then she smiled. "It looks just like the picture in my coloring book. It looks like Paris."

"It *is* Paris," Paul said. He seemed pleased. "My mom bought these toys for me in France."

For a moment Nancy forgot about the mystery she had to solve. She knelt down next to Paul. "You know what you need?" she said. "An Eiffel Tower."

Paul raced another car past a traffic light. "I have one of those somewhere," he said, without looking up.

"It would make the scene so perfect," said Nancy. "Is your tower in here?" She reached for Paul's toy box.

Paul's head snapped up. He grabbed the box and held it close. "Don't touch!" he cried.

Nancy backed away a few inches. Then she jumped up and raced past Paul toward the theater. She wanted to search for the tape one last time. She hurried through the backstage door.

The lights were on, and someone was whistling. Nancy followed the tune and saw Jerry Cutter. He was sweeping

near the sound system. He looked cheerful.

"Hi," Nancy said.

Jerry waved and grinned at Nancy. "I hope you're not planning to practice backstage," he said. "I'm closing up in a minute. Then I'm out of here."

"I guess you're pretty happy," Nancy said. "The recital's going to be canceled. You can go to the Creeps concert."

Jerry shook his head. "The recital isn't a problem for me. The guy who works the lights didn't have the flu after all. He called Madame Dugrand yesterday."

Nancy had a sinking feeling in her stomach. "You mean you don't care if we have the recital?"

Jerry looked surprised. "Sure I care," he said. "I wish you girls *could* have it. You've worked hard. It's really rotten that someone took that tape."

Nancy didn't answer. There goes my last suspect, she thought. And there goes my last chance to solve this mystery.

Jerry was sweeping again—this time

under the sound system. "Look at that," he said. He pointed his broom at something on the floor. "I'd get my work done a lot faster if you kids didn't eat so much junk food."

Nancy peered at the floor. She saw some broken potato chips. Mixed in with them were several small, round, red candies.

"Hot Shots," Nancy murmured.

She kept looking at the candies.

"Hey, are you all right?" Jerry asked.

Nancy didn't hear him. She unzipped her dance bag and took out her notebook and pen. On the page of suspects she crossed out Jerry Cutter's name. Under her Eiffel Tower picture she wrote: "Hot Shots." Then she put the notebook and pen away. She took out the Eiffel Tower charm and held it in her hand.

Suddenly Nancy looked up. "I've got it!" she shouted. "I've got it!"

"Got what?" Jerry asked.

He didn't get an answer. Nancy was already racing for the door.

Out in the hallway Nancy dashed

toward Paul. She glanced at the clock beyond him. Ten minutes to three!

"Paul," Nancy said. "Is this yours?" She held out the Eiffel Tower charm.

Paul looked at the charm and nodded. Nancy handed it to him. Then she walked past all his toys and turned the corner.

A noisy crowd of girls was standing at the other end of the hallway. Some were near Madame's office. Others were outside the dressing room and the practice studio.

Nancy's heart was pounding. I know who took the tape! she thought. And I think I know where it is. But how can I prove it? How can I get the tape back?

Darcy Blair stepped out of Madame's office. "Quiet, everyone!" she called out. The noise began to die down. "Madame wants you all in the practice studio. Let's go!"

Nancy turned to look at the clock. Five minutes to three. Madame was about to cancel the recital!

Nancy noticed Bess and George in

the crowd of girls. Then she got an idea.

Nancy dashed down the hall. She pulled Bess and George aside.

"There's no time to explain," she whispered. "But I can solve the mystery—if you help me. I'll tell you what to do."

The three girls headed up the hall. Nancy gave Bess and George directions as fast as she could. "I don't like to trick anyone," Nancy said. "But it's our only chance."

When they reached the corner, Nancy stopped. She moved close to the wall so that she could listen. Bess and George walked around the corner.

"Hi, Paul," Nancy heard George say. "Are you coming to the practice studio?"

"What for?" Paul asked.

"Your mom is going to make a big announcement," Bess said. "She's found the tape. Why don't you come and hear?"

A few seconds later Bess and George walked back around the corner. They hurried toward the practice studio. As they passed Nancy, George gave her a thumbs-up sign.

Nancy slowly peeked around the corner. She saw Paul grab his toy box and yank off the lid. He looked worried. He dug down into the box and pulled something out.

Nancy stepped around the corner. She spoke in a soft but clear voice.

"Paul, that's the missing tape!"

8

Let the Ballet Begin!

George and Bess reached the studio door. Madame was just about to go in. She held the door open for them. Then she stepped inside.

A hush fell over the studio. For once Madame didn't smile at her students. Her eyes weren't twinkling. She glanced at her watch.

"It's three o'clock," she said. "I'm afraid I have a sad announcement to make. Our recital is can—"

The door swung open. Nancy rushed

in. "Madame!" she said. Every pair of eyes turned to Nancy. "I found the tape!"

"You found it!" Madame repeated. "Where?"

"You have to come into the hallway," Nancy said. "Alone."

Madame followed Nancy into the hallway. She shut the studio door. Paul was leaning against the wall. When he saw his mother, his eyes filled with tears. He held out the tape.

"Paul!" Madame gasped. "What happened?"

Paul jabbed the toe of his sneaker against the floor a few times. When he finally spoke, his voice was very low.

"I hate the stupid recital! I hate the rehearsals!" A tear rolled down each cheek.

Madame knelt next to Paul. She put her arm around his shoulders. "So you took the tape," she said quietly.

Paul nodded.

"You shouldn't have done that," Madame said. "And I think you know it.

But I made a mistake, too. I didn't see how upset you were after your baby-sitter quit."

Paul put his arms around his mother's neck. "I'm sorry I took the tape," he said softly.

Madame gave him a kiss. "We will talk more later. And we won't let anything like this happen again," she said. "I promise."

Then she stood up and spoke to Nancy. "Thank you for solving the mystery." Madame laughed and gave Nancy a hug. "You're quite a detective. You did just what you said you wanted to do. You saved the recital!"

Nancy looked at herself in the back-stage mirror. In just fifteen minutes the recital would begin. Under the lights her silvery green leotard and tights glittered. She straightened the elastic on her ballet slippers.

Bess stood on Nancy's right. She re-tied a green ribbon in her hair. George stood on Nancy's left. She was bounc-

ing up and down on her toes. All their
eyes met in the mirror. The three
friends burst into giggles.

"Now I have two *zillion* butterflies in
my stomach," Bess moaned. "I'm so
nervous!"

"I can't stand still!" said George.

"Me, either," Nancy said. "But we
shouldn't be nervous. We all did okay
in the dress rehearsal this afternoon.
The recital is just like the dress rehearsal, right?"

"Wrong!" Bess said. "All those people will be watching us." She pretended to shiver.

"Hey, you three are hogging the
mirror," someone behind them com-
plained.

Nancy turned around. It was Brenda
Carlton. But she didn't look angry.

"It's all yours," Nancy said. Then she
noticed Alison standing next to Brenda.
"Good luck with your solo," Nancy
added.

"Thanks," Alison said. "I'm so
scared. I think I'll need some luck."

69

"Me, too," Rebecca Ramirez said. She and Jessie Shapiro were standing behind Alison.

"Feel my hands," Jessie said, pressing Bess's hands in her own. "They're freezing."

"Eeeek!" Bess screamed. "They're ice!"

Nancy, Bess, and George ducked through the crowd of girls around the mirror.

"Let's find a quiet place to wait," Nancy suggested.

She glanced around backstage. There were mermaids, fairies, and pirates everywhere. All the dancers were whispering and giggling. Madame Dugrand and Darcy were checking costumes and makeup for the last time.

"Over there," Nancy said. She pointed to the curtain.

The girls found some space in the wings just to the side of the stage.

"Now tell us," George said to Nancy.

Nancy grinned. "Tell you what?"

Bess rolled her eyes. "The mystery!

How did you know Paul Dugrand took the tape?"

Nancy's eyes sparkled. "I saw Jerry Cutter sweep up some cinnamon candies near the sound system. Then I remembered that Paul was eating cinnamon candy Hot Shots on Friday night—right before we knew the tape was missing."

"And what about the Eiffel Tower charm?" Bess asked.

"Paul told me he had an Eiffel Tower," Nancy explained. "Then I guessed that he could have dropped the candy *and* the charm when he took the tape."

"Pretty smart!" George said. "But how did you guess where he hid the tape?"

"I tried to touch his toy box," Nancy said. "He grabbed it away from me. It seemed like he was hiding something."

"You really are a detective," Bess said. "You saved me from total doom."

"Sh-sh-sh!" Darcy Blair hurried over to the girls. She held a finger to her lips.

"The audience will hear you," she whispered. "Now, let's see how you look."

Darcy checked their costumes and makeup. "George needs blush and lipstick," she said.

"No way!" George muttered. Then she whispered to Nancy, "Save *me* from total doom."

"I need more blush, too," Bess said.

Darcy looked at Bess's face. "You're a mermaid, not a tomato. Remember?"

"Please," Bess begged.

Darcy laughed. "Just a tiny bit."

As Darcy put more blush on Bess's cheeks, George tried to slip behind the deep folds of the curtain.

"George Fayne!" Darcy said in a loud whisper. "Come back here!"

Darcy dabbed some makeup on George's face. George stood with her hands clenched, shoulders scrunched up, and eyes closed. Nancy and Bess couldn't help laughing.

"You look like you're swallowing rotten fish medicine," Nancy said.

"Total doom!" George muttered.

Madame clapped her hands. Everyone knew what that meant. The recital was about to start! Nancy, George, and Bess ran to get in line with the other mermaids.

Madame and Darcy bustled all the dancers onstage. When they were in position, Darcy went back to the sound system. Madame stood in the wings.

Nancy faced the curtain. She could hear the loud hum of the audience talking. She could hear their programs rustling.

"Dim the house lights," Madame said.

The theater grew still. The butterflies in Nancy's stomach fluttered faster than ever. She took a deep breath. She, Bess, and George squeezed hands for a second.

"Good luck!" Nancy whispered.

Madame tapped her foot and then counted. "One. Two. *Three!*"

The music began. It was the opening song for "Scenes from Peter Pan."

The curtain rose.

An hour later the students of Madame Dugrand's Dance Academy took their final bow. The audience was clapping. Some people shouted "Bravo!"

Nancy bowed just the way Madame had taught them. She held out her right leg, toe pointed. She bent her left knee.

The curtain dropped.

"We did it!" Bess cheered.

Nancy, Bess, and George hugged one another. They couldn't stop laughing.

"That was fun!" George said.

"Fun and scary!" Bess added. "I almost fainted when I saw my parents in the audience."

"Everyone, backstage!" Madame called. She looked just as happy as her dancers. She noticed Bess. "You did very well, dear."

Bess nodded. "I made only one mistake. A really little one."

Madame patted Nancy's shoulder. "Thank you again," she said.

When Nancy got backstage, her father was already there.

"Signorina Ballerina!" he sang out. Then he handed Nancy a bunch of

pink roses. They were tied with a big pink bow.

"Wow! Roses!" Nancy said. She hugged her father.

"And now, how about some ice cream?" Carson Drew asked. "Change out of your costume. We can meet Bess, George, and their families at Sugar 'n' Spice."

Nancy nodded happily. "But I have to do one thing first," she said. "It won't take long."

Nancy hurried to a corner near the sound system. She'd left her dance bag there. She got out her blue notebook and turned to a clean page. Then she wrote:

Friends can solve sticky problems if they stick together. I found the missing tape. Now no one thinks Bess took it. We helped her practice the dance, and she learned the steps.

Being a ballerina has been lots of fun—almost as much fun as being a detective!

Case closed.